THE HUNDRED HEADLESS WOMAN

THE HUNDRED HEADLESS WOMAN

(*La femme 100 têtes*)

MAX ERNST

Foreword by André Breton

George Braziller / New York

For information address the publisher:
George Braziller, Inc.
One Park Avenue
New York, N.Y. 10016

Library of Congress Catalog Card Number: 81-67737

ISBN 0-8076-1023-2 (cloth)
      0-8076-1024-0 (paper)

Designer: Peter McKenzie

1st American Edition
Printed in the United States

FOREWORD

The splendid illustrations of novels and children's books like *Rocambole* or *Costal the Indian*, intended for persons who can scarcely read, are among the few things capable of moving to tears those who can say they have read everything. This road to knowledge, which tends to substitute the most forbidding, mirageless desert for the most astonishing virgin-forest, is not, unhappily, of the sort that permits retreat. The most we can hope for is to peek into some old gilt-edged volume, some pages with turned-down corners (as if we were only allowed to find the magician's hat), sparkling or somber pages that might reveal better than all else the special nature of our dreams, the elective reality of our love, the manner of our life's incomparable unwinding. And if such is the way a soul is formed, how would one view the ordinary simple soul that is daily formed by sight and sound rather than texts, that needs the massive shock of the sight of blood, the ceremonious blacks and whites, the ninety-degree angle of spring light, the miracles found in trash, the popular songs; of that candid soul that vibrates in millions and that on the day of revolution, and just because of that simple candor, will carve its true emblems in the unalterable colors of its own exaltation. These colors that are all we want to remember of the anthems, golden chalices, gunfire, waving plumes and banners, even when they are absent from these pages, pages forming a luminous bouquet above a far-away phrase ("Shoking cried: Peace, Sultan!" or "His half-open coat disclosed a lamp hanging from his neck" or "All seized their swords in the same instant") suspended from a phrase waking the echoes of the *passé défini*—for some

7

reason ever more mysterious—are, for better or worse, from birth to death, the colors that dye our enchantment and our fear. Spoken or written language cannot describe an event in the way it brings about the highly suggestive and furtive displacements of animate or inanimate beings, and it is patently evident that one can't give even a hint of a character while trying to lend him some interest without revealing his full portrait. How not to deplore then the fact that until now only rather flat adventure stories have been the object of the kind of inquiry that occupies us here, and that even now most of the artists charged with giving greater value to tales which, without their intervention would remain ephemeral, have not hesitated to deflect attention from that which occurs by the author's intention and instead bring it to focus on their "style"? Thus one can proclaim the genius of those anonymous illustrators of *The Chronicle of the Duke Ernst* and *Fantômas* in their whole-hearted submission to the faintest caprices of a text or their enthusiastic search for the tone to which a work aspires.

It remained to examine these grid-covered pages*, out of a thousand old books with all kinds of titles, of forgotten identity—by which I mean that they are no longer read. These illustrations, unlike the impossibly boring texts they refer to, represent for us a plethora of such disconcerting conjectures that they become precious in themselves, as is the meticulous reconstruction of a crime witnessed in a dream, without our being in the least concerned with the name or motives of the assassin. Many of these pictures, full of an agitation all the more extraordinary for its cause being unknown to us—and the case is the same with diagrams from, say, some technical work, providing we know nothing of it—give an illusion of veritable *slits* in time, space, customs and even beliefs, wherein there is not one element that isn't finally a risk, and whose use, to fulfill even the elastic conditions of verisimilitude, would be unthinkable for any other purpose: this man with white beard coming out of a house holding a lantern, if I cover the rest with my hand, might find himself face to face with a winged lion; if I cover his lantern he might just as easily, thus posed, drop stars or stones to the ground. Superposition, if I am

*Reference is made here to the process of engraving, the only means of reproducing pictures until the advent of photography. (Translator's note.)

not careful, and even if I am, operates moreover, if not strictly speaking before our eyes, at least very objectively and in a continuous manner. This marvelous array, that skips pages as a little girl skips rope or traces a magic circle to use as a hoop, roams day and night the warehouse where all those things we involuntarily accept or reject are stored in the greatest disorder. Each one's special truth is a game of solitaire in which he must quickly choose his cards from among all the others and without ever having seen them before.

Everything that has been written about, described, called fake, doubtful, or true, and above all, pictured, has a singular power to touch us: it is clear that we can't possess it all and so desire it all the more. The wisest of men tends to play with some grave science or other almost as with the evanescent images of a flickering fireplace. History itself, with the childish impressions that it leaves in our minds—more likely of Charles VI or Geneviève de Brabant than of Mary Stuart or Louis XIV—history falls *outside* like snow.

One awaited a book that would take into account the drastic exaggeration of those salient lines emphasized by the attenuation of all the others, a book whose author had the drive needed to bring him to the top of the precipice of indifference where a statue is far less interesting on its pedestal than in a pit, where an aurora borealis reproduced in the magazine *Nature* is less beautiful than in any unexpected elsewhere. Surreality will be, moreover, the means of our wish for total evasion (and it is understood that one can go so far in dislocating a hand from its arm that the hand thereby becomes increasingly *hand*, and also that in speaking of evasion we are not only referring to space). We awaited a book that avoids all parallels with other books aside from their mutual use of ink and type, as if there were the slightest need, in making a statue appear in a pit, to be the sculptor! I would add, besides, that in order to be truly displaced, the statue had to have once lived a conventional statue-life in a conventional statue-place. The entire value of such an enterprise—and perhaps of all artistic enterprise—seems to me a question of choice*, of audacity and of the success, by one's power of

---

*"Taste" is the literal word used here. I have preferred "choice" as reflecting, in English, the truer thought of André Breton. (Translator's note.)

appropriation, of certain *transformations*. One awaited a book that refused at once the mysterious, the troubled qualities of many universes that are similar by virtue only of a rather meaningless physio-moral principle and are, to say the least, undesirable in any sense of grandeur (let's take a bottle: *they* immediately think we are about to drink, but no, it is empty, corked, and bobbing on the waves; now *they*'ve got it: it is the bottle on the sea, and so on). Everything has a use other than the one generally attributed to it. It is even out of the conscious sacrifice of their primary usage (to manipulate an object for the first time not knowing what is or was its use) that certain transcendent properties can be deduced, properties that belong to another given or possible world where, for example, an axe can be taken for a sunset, where the virtual elements are not even admissible (I imagine a phantom at a crossroads consulting the road sign), where the migratory instinct usually attributed to birds, encompasses autumn leaves, where former lives, actual lives, future lives melt together into one life; the *life* utterly depersonalized (what a pity for the painters: never to be able to make more than one or two heads; and the novelists! Only human beings do not resemble each other). One awaited, finally, *The Hundred Headless Woman* because one knew that in our day Max Ernst is the only one to have severely refused those considerations that for other artists refer to "form," in regard to which all compliance leads to chanting the idiotic hymn of the "three apples" perpetrated, in the final analysis, all the more grotesquely for their manners, by Cézanne and Renoir. Because one knew that Max Ernst was not the man to draw back from anything that might widen the modern field of vision and provoke the innumerable *illusions of true recognition* that we alone must choose to see in the future and in the past. Because one knew that Max Ernst's is the most magnificently haunted brain of our day, by that I mean the one that knows it is not enough to send a new boat into the world, even a pirate ship, but instead to build the *ark* and in such a way that, this time, it is not the dove that returns, but the raven.

The Hundred Headless Woman will be preeminently the picture book of our day, wherein it will be more and more apparent that every living room has gone "to the bottom of a lake" with, we must point out, its chandeliers of fishes, its gilded stars, its dancing grasses, its mud bottom and its raiment of reflections. Such is our idea of progress that, on the eve of 1930, we are glad and impatient, for once, to see children's eyes, filled with the ineffable, open like butterflies on the edge of this lake while, for their amazement and our own, fall the black lace masks that covered the first hundred faces of the enchantress.

1929   —ANDRÉ BRETON

(*Translation by* DOROTHEA TANNING)

To Max

Here is *La Femme 100 Têtes*, *The Hundred Headless Woman*, rendered into English. I know you would be glad to see it brought, with its trail of dazzling light, and dark, to all those who never saw it before. That means a whole world full of new people. They will make an intoxicating discovery of surreal experience which, contrary to the general notion that surreal rhymes with dream, will reveal a quite undreamlike toughness of muscle, a tide of metaphor incised like the engraver's lines on our copper days and noisy nights; an experience that will whip the mind into a shape of resistance to our human quagmire.

When I first saw *The Hundred Headless Woman* I was not prepared for such a banquet. It took several meetings to savor it fully and even now there is no use pretending that I have plumbed it all.

As Loplop, Bird-Superior, you hatched her in Paris in 1927. "Perturbation, my sister," "she keeps her secret," "the torpid train," are talismanic phrases that chart the gazer's progress through this easy, liberated world where everything is possible.

The Hundred Headless Woman has a hundred heads and no head at all, and we are certain that nothing could be more fitting. Levitation is the order of the day. She knows no boundaries, no gravity, no laws. I see her in the turmoil of phenomenal rooms and tangled silences, or out there in the vastness with you and the other comets, crossing the sky, on friendly terms with the universe. Alas, we cannot join you. But we can guess at your course.

DOROTHEA

CHAPTER ONE

Crime ou miracle : un homme complet.

Crime or miracle: a complete man.

L'immaculée conception manquée.

The might-have-been Immaculate Conception.

La même, pour la deuxième...

The same, for the second . . .

. . . et la troisième fois manquée.

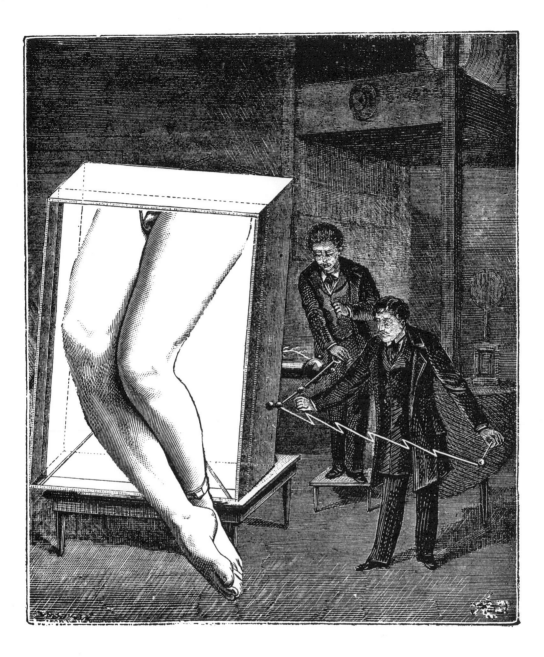

. . . and the third time missed.

Le paysage change trois fois (I).

The landscape changes 3 times (I).

Le paysage change trois fois (II).

The landscape changes 3 times (II).

Le paysage change trois fois (III).

The landscape changes 3 times (III).

L'agneau demi-fécond dilate son abdomen à volonté et devient agnelle.

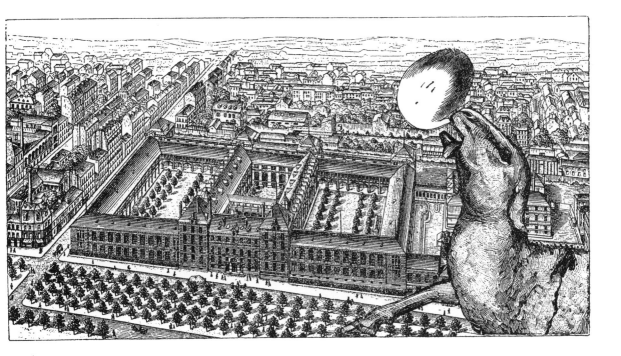

The demi-fecond ram dilates its abdomen at will and becomes a ewe.

Le ciel se découvre deux fois (I).

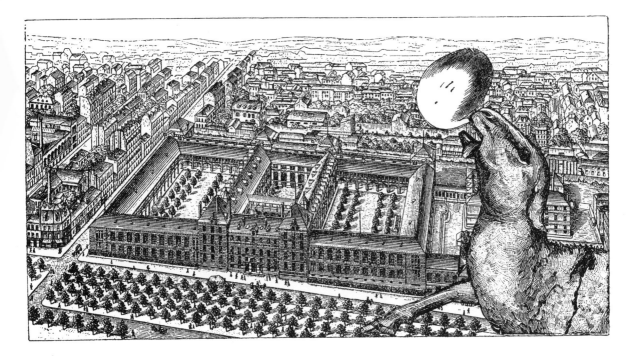

The demi-fecond ram dilates its abdomen at will and becomes a ewe.

Le ciel se découvre deux fois (I).

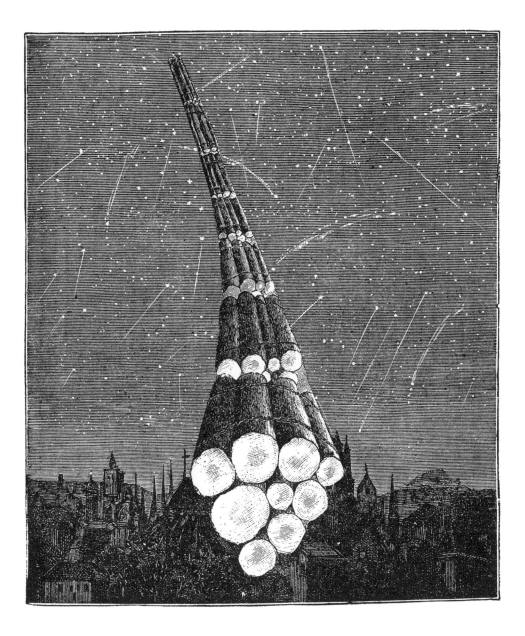

The sky opens twice (I).

Le ciel se découvre deux fois (II).

The sky opens twice (II).

Dans le bassin de Paris, Loplop, le supérieur des oiseaux, apporte
aux réverbères la nourriture nocturne.

In the heart of Paris, Loplop, Bird-Superior, brings nightly food
to the streetlamps.

L'immaculée conception.

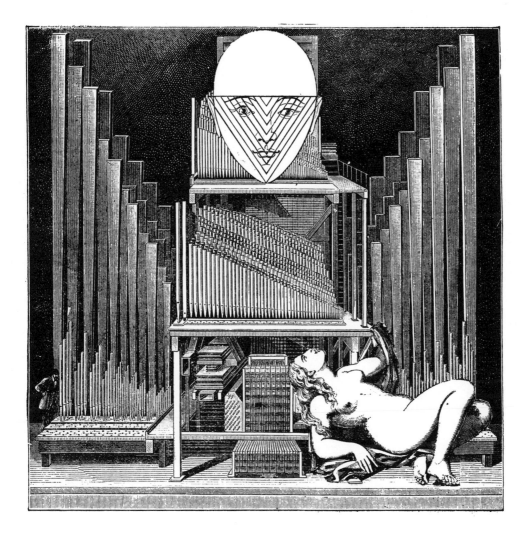

The Immaculate Conception.

CHAPTER TWO

A plus tendre jeunesse, extrême onction.

To tenderest youth, extreme unction.

Le grand saint Nicolas est suivi d'impeccables parasites et guidé à distance par ses deux appendices latéraux.

The great St. Nicholas is followed by impassable parasites and teleguided
by his two lateral appendages.

A bébé éventré, pigeonnier ouvert.

Eviscerated baby, open dove-cote.

Où l'on voit apparaître un charmant petit insecte à cheveux métalliques.

Where you can see a charming little insect with metallic hair.

L'inconscience du paysage devient complète.

The unconsciousness of the landscape becomes complete.

Ici se préparent les premières touches de la grâce et les jeux sans issue.

The first touches of grace and the unresolved games are being prepared here.

On augmentera par des lessives bouillantes le charme des transports
et blessures en silence.

The charm of transportations and wounds will be increased in silence
by boiling laundry.

Suite des jeux diurnes, crépusculaires et nocturnes.

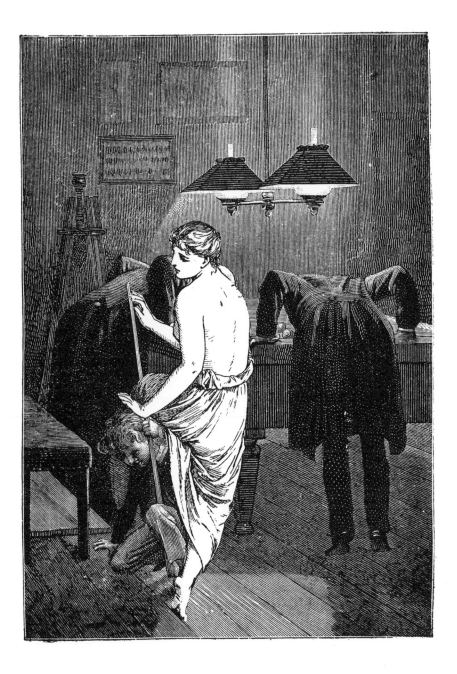

Continuation of morning, twilight and night games.

Suite.

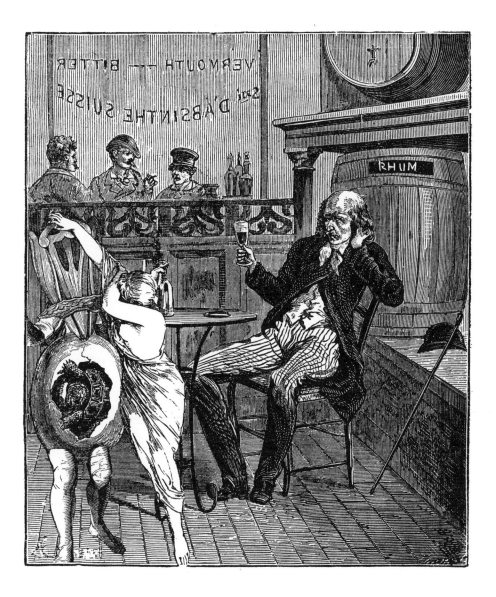

Continuation.

Odeur de fleurs sèches, ou : Je veux être reine de Saba.

Odor of dried flowers, or: I want to be Queen of Sheba.

Germinal, ma sœur, la femme 100 têtes. (Au fond, dans la cage, le Père Éternel.)

Germinal, my sister, the hundred headless woman. (In the background, in the cage, the Eternal Father.)

Nouvelle suite des jeux diurnes, crépusculaires et nocturnes.

New series of morning, twilight and night games.

Suite.

Continuation.

Suite.

Continuation.

Suite.

Continuation.

Pendant le jour, les caresses angéliques se retirent dans les régions secrètes, voisines des pôles.

During the day, angelic caresses hide in secret regions,
adjacent to the poles.

Suite.

Continuation.

Fête rangée en bracelet autour des branches.

Festival hung like a bracelet around the branches.

Prométhée.

Prometheus.

La femme 100 têtes ouvre sa manche auguste.

The hundred headless woman opens her august sleeve.

Ce singe, serait-il catholique, par hasard?

This monkey, would he be catholic by any chance?

Perturbation, ma sœur, la femme 100 têtes.

Perturbation, my sister, the hundred headless woman.

L'exorbitante récompense.

The exorbitant reward.

CHAPTER THREE

Sans souffler mot et par n'importe quel temps, lumière magique.

Without uttering a word and in all kinds of weather, magic light.

Leçons obscures.

Obscure lessons.

Stridulations des fantômes du dimanche.

Loud chirpings of Sunday phantoms.

La même.

The same.

On voit filer plus d'un notaire laissant tomber sa voix en cadence.

One sees more than one notary pass by, letting his voice fall in cadences.

Loplop et l'horoscope de la souris.

Loplop and the mouse's horoscope.

La troisième souris assise, on voit voler le corps d'une adulte légendaire.

With the third mouse seated, one sees the flying body of a legendary adult.

Alors je vous présenterai l'oncle dont, les dimanches après-midi,
nous aimions chatouiller la barbe.

Then let me present the uncle whose beard we liked to tickle
on Sunday afternoons.

L'oncle à peine étranglé, la jeune adulte sans pareille s'envole.

The moment the uncle is strangled, the matchless young adult flies away.

Sorcellerie ou quelque farce macabre.

Sorcery, or some macabre farce.

Un cri de grand diamètre étouffe les fruits et morceaux de viande
dans leur cercueil.

A scream of large diameter stifles the fruit and the pieces of meat
in the coffin.

On débute alors par une petite fête en famille.

Then one begins with a little family party.

Culture physique, ou : la mort qu'il vous plaira.

Physical culture, or: the death you prefer.

Les hivernants de la Grande Jatte.

The Grande Jatte hibernators.

Enregistrement de bagage vaut titre de noblesse.

Baggage check-in is worth a title of nobility.

Le train engourdi.

The torpid train.

Défais ton sac, mon brave.

Open your bag, my good man.

Yachting.

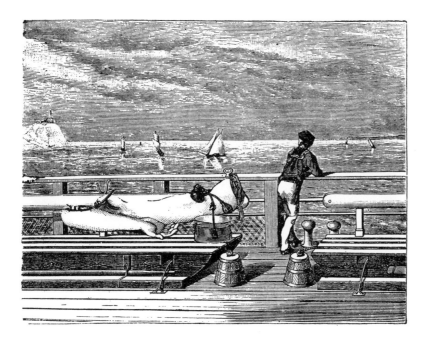

Yachting.

La sève monte.

The sap rises.

Loplop, l'hirondelle, passe.

Loplop, the swallow, passes by.

Se nourrissant souvent de rêves liquides et tout à fait semblables à des feuilles endormies, voici mes sept sœurs ensemble.

Here all together are my seven sisters, often living on liquid dreams
and perfectly resembling sleeping leaves.

Loplop, l'hirondelle, revient.

Loplop, the swallow, returns.

Loplop, le supérieur des oiseaux, effarouche les derniers vestiges
de la dévotion en commun.

Loplop, Bird Superior, chases away the last vestiges
of group devotion.

Le sphinx et le pain quotidien font une visite au couvent.

The sphinx and the daily bread visit the convent.

Le Père Éternel, la barbe sillonnée d'éclairs continus, dans une catastrophe de métro.

The Eternal Father, his beard laced with continuous lightning, in a subway accident.

Loplop et la Belle Jardinière.

Loplop and the beautiful gardener.

Presque seule avec les fantômes et les fourmis : Germinal, ma sœur,
la femme 100 têtes.

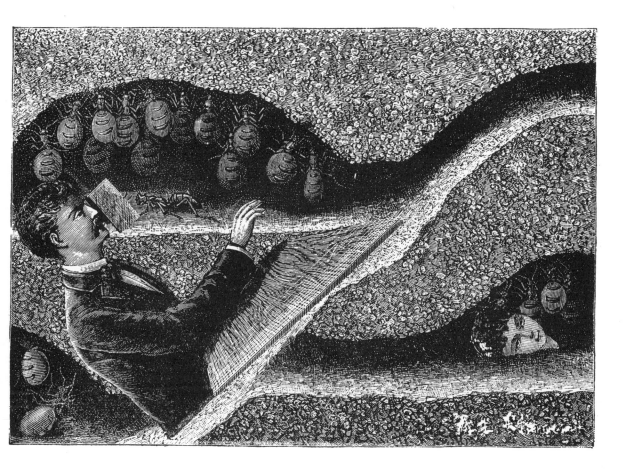

Almost alone with the ghosts and the ants: Germinal, my sister,
the hundred headless woman.

La lune est belle.

The moon is beautiful.

Et les femmes volcaniques relèvent et agitent, d'un air menaçant,
la partie postérieure de leur corps.

And volcanic women lift and shake their bodies' posterior parts
in a menacing way.

CHAPTER FOUR

Nul objet n'arrêtera ce sourire de passage qui accompagne les crimes d'un sexe à l'autre.

Nothing will stop this passing smile which accompanies heterosexual crimes.

Dans la roue dite du Poison, rencontres illimitées et robustes effervescences.

Unlimited meetings and robust effervescences in the wheel known as Poison.

Décharge publique, ou : toutes les escales se valent.

Public garbage dump, or: all the pauses are equally worthwhile.

Et Loplop, le supérieur des oiseaux, s'est fait chair sans chair et habitera parmi nous.

And Loplop, Bird-Superior, has transformed himself into flesh without flesh
and will dwell among us.

Son sourire sera d'une sobre élégance.

His smile will be of a sober elegance.

Son arme sera l'ivresse, sa morsure le feu.

His arm will be intoxication, his bite will be fire.

Son regard s'enfoncera tout droit dans les débris des villes desséchées.

His gaze will penetrate the debris of dried-up cities.

Vivant seule sur son globe-fantôme, belle et parée de ses rêves : Perturbation, ma sœur, la femme 100 têtes.

Living alone on her phantom globe, beautiful and dressed in her dreams:
Perturbation, my sister, the hundred headless woman.

Chaque émeute sanglante la fera vivre pleine de grâce et de vérité.

Each bloody riot will help her to live in grace and truth.

Son sourire, le feu, tombera sous forme de gelée noire et de rouille blanche
sur les flancs de la montagne.

Her smile of fire will fall on the mountain sides in the form
of black jelly and white rust.

Et son globe-fantôme nous retrouvera . . .

And her phantom globe will track us down . . .

. . . à toutes les escales.

. . . at every stop.

CHAPTER FIVE

Plus légère que l'atmosphère, puissante et isolée : Perturbation, ma sœur, la femme 100 têtes.

Lighter than air, strong and isolated: Perturbation, my sister,
the hundred headless woman.

Mais les flots sont amers.

But the waves are bitter.

La vérité restera simple et des roues gigantesques sillonneront les flots amers.

Truth will remain simple, and gigantic wheels will ride the bitter waves.

Et les images s'abaisseront jusqu'au sol.

And images will descend to the ground.

Tous les vendredis, les Titans parcourront nos buanderies d'un vol rapide
avec de fréquents crochets.

Every Friday, in rapid flight and with frequent detours,
Titans will invade our laundries.

Et rien ne sera plus commun qu'un Titan au restaurant.

And no sight will be more common than a Titan in the restaurant.

Dans la cécité des charrons on trouvera le germe de bien précieuses visions.

One will discover the germ of very precious visions in the blindness of wheelwrights.

Les forgerons gris, noirs ou volcaniques, tournoieront dans l'air au-dessus
des forges et . . .

Gray, black or volcanic blacksmiths will whirl in the air
over the forges and . . .

. . . forgeront des couronnes d'autant plus larges qu'ils s'élèveront plus haut.

. . . will forge crowns so large that they will rise higher.

Plus puissante que les volcans, légère et isolée : Perturbation, ma sœur,
la femme 100 têtes.

Stronger than volcanoes, airy and isolated, Perturbation, my sister,
the hundred headless woman.

Perturbation, élévation, abaissement.

Perturbation, elevation, diminution.

Roulement de tambours dans les pierres.

Drum-roll among the stones.

Dilapidations, aurore et fantôme méticuleux à l'excès.

Dilapidation, dawn and excessively meticulous phantom.

La tranquillité des assassinats anciens . . .

The tranquillity of ancient assassinations . . .

. . . et futurs.

. . . and future ones.

Pièces à conviction.

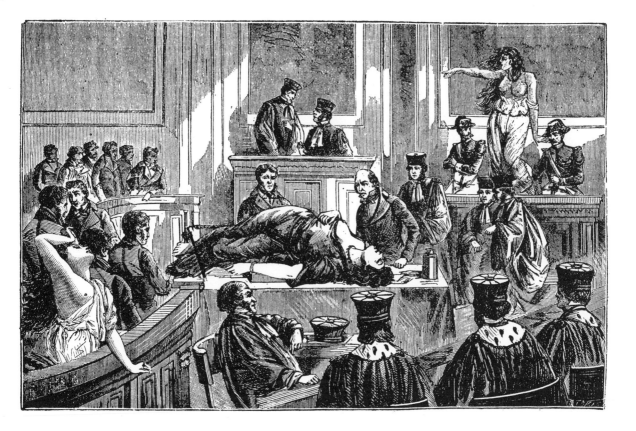

Material evidence.

CHAPTER SIX

Le départ pour la pêche miraculeuse.

Departure for the miraculous catch.

Plus isolée que la mer, toujours légère et puissante : Perturbation, ma sœur, la femme 100 têtes.

More isolated than the sea, still airy and powerful: Perturbation, my sister,
the hundred headless woman.

Voici la soif qui me ressemble.

Here is the thirst that resembles me.

La pêche miraculeuse, clameurs et amour.

The miraculous fish, noise and love.

Le tonnerre jubilant et gracieux, maître de la nuit.

Jubilant and gracious thunder, master of night.

La mer de la sérénité.

Sea of serenity.

Le geste élégant du noyé.

The elegant gesture of the drowned.

Quiétude.

Quietude.

La mer de la Jubilation.

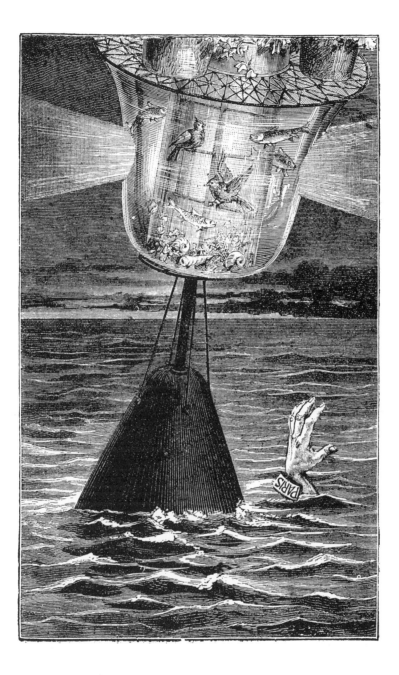

Sea of jubilation.

CHAPTER SEVEN

La nuit hurle dans sa retraite et s'approche de nos yeux comme de la chair à vif.

Night screams in her lair and approaches our eyes like raw flesh.

Entraînée par le silence, une porte s'ouvre à reculons.

Seduced by the silence, a door opens backwards.

Un corps sans corps se place parallèlement à son corps et nous indique tel un fantôme sans fantôme, au moyen d'une salive particulière, la matrice servant à faire les timbres-poste.

A body without a body lies down beside its body and, like a phantom
without a phantom, and with a special saliva, shows us the way to the
womb that serves to make postage stamps.

Deux corps sans corps se placent parallèlement à leur corps en tombant du lit et des rideaux, tels des fantômes sans fantôme.

Two bodies without bodies lie down alongside their bodies, falling
out of bed and bed-curtains like phantoms without a phantom.

La femme 100 têtes irait jusqu'à sourire en dormant pour que Loplop
sourit aux fantômes.

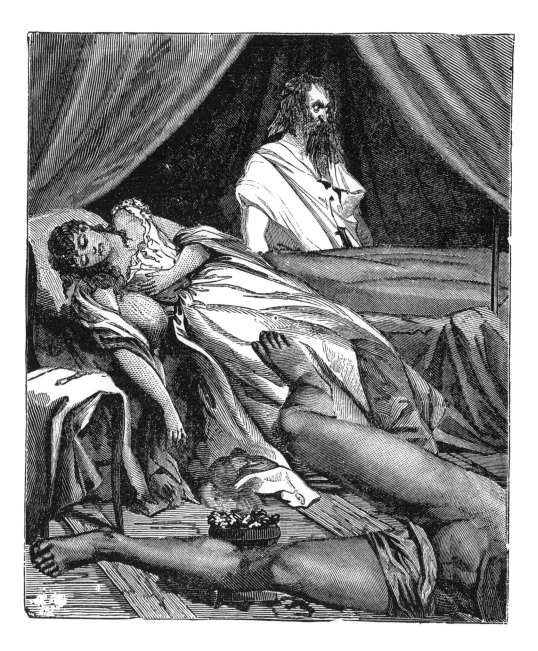

The hundred headless woman will even smile in her sleep in order that Loplop
will smile at the phantoms.

Loplop, ivre de peur et de fureur, retrouve sa tête d'oiseau et reste
immobile pendant 12 jours des deux côtés de la porte.

Loplop, dumb with fear and fury, finds his bird head and remains motionless
for 12 days on both sides of the door.

La forêt s'écarte alors devant un couple accompli suivi d'un corps aveugle.

Then the forest makes way for a united couple followed by a blind body.

Pour évoquer le septième âge qui succède à la neuvième naissance, Germinal aux yeux invisibles, la lune et Loplop décrivent des ovales avec leur tête.

Germinal of the invisible eyes, the moon, and Loplop describe ovals with their heads
so as to call up the seventh age following the ninth birth.

A ce moment, les fantômes entrent dans la période de voracité.

At this moment the phantoms enter their voracious period.

Tantôt nus, tantôt vêtus de minces jets de feu, ils font gicler les geysers avec la probabilité d'une pluie de sang et avec la vanité des morts.

Sometimes naked, sometimes dressed in thin jets of fire, they cause the geysers to spurt
with the probability of a rain of blood and with the vanity of the dead.

A la lueur de leurs écailles, ils préfèrent la poussière des tapis à la masturbation des feuilles fraîches, les pieux mensonges.

In the light of their scales they prefer rug dust to masturbation of
fresh leaves, pious lies.

Mais ils s'éloignent avec crainte, dès que des roulements de tambour se font entendre
sous l'eau.

But they leave fearfully when the drum-roll is heard
under the water.

Et ils ramassent au hasard quelques gâteaux secs dans les creux de la Chaussée des Géants. Celle-ci est un amas de berceaux.

And they pick up random cookies in the hollow of Giants' Road:
this is a pile of cradles.

. . . .

. . . . .

. . . . .

. . . . .

CHAPTER EIGHT

Reste donc celui qui spécule sur la vanité des morts, le fantôme
de la repopulation.

So he who speculates on the vanity of the dead remains the phantom
of repopulation.

Toutes les portes se ressemblent.

All doors look alike.

Et les papillons se mettent à chanter.

And the butterflies begin to sing.

Parmi les fantômes faisant partie de ce chapitre . . .

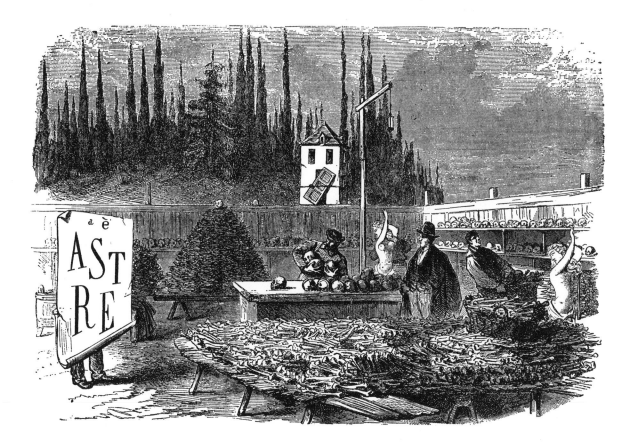

Among the phantoms in this chapter . . .

. . . on reconnaîtra . . .

. . . one recognizes . . .

. . . après une légère hésitation . . . .

. . . after a slight hesitation . . . .

Pasteur dans son cabinet de travail.

Pasteur in his laboratory.

Le singe qui sera policier, catholique ou boursier.

The monkey who will be a policeman, a catholic, or a broker.

Fantômas, Dante et Jules Verne.

Fantômas, Dante and Jules Verne.

Cézanne et Rosa Bonheur.

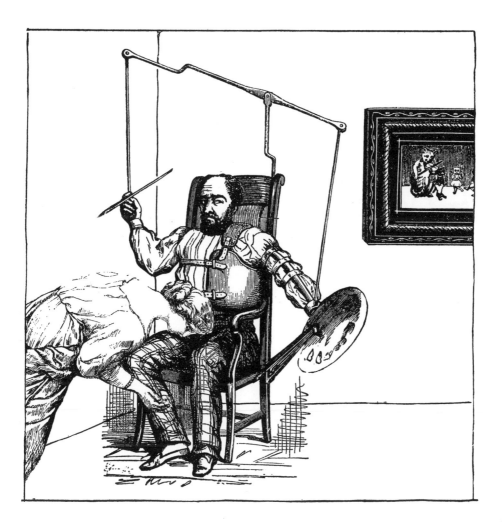

Cézanne and Rosa Bonheur.

Mata Hari.

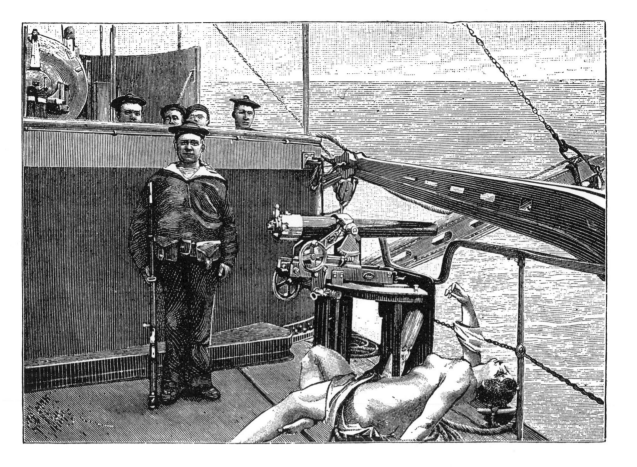

Mata Hari.

Saint Lazare, glorieusement ressuscité de la fiente des dromadaires.

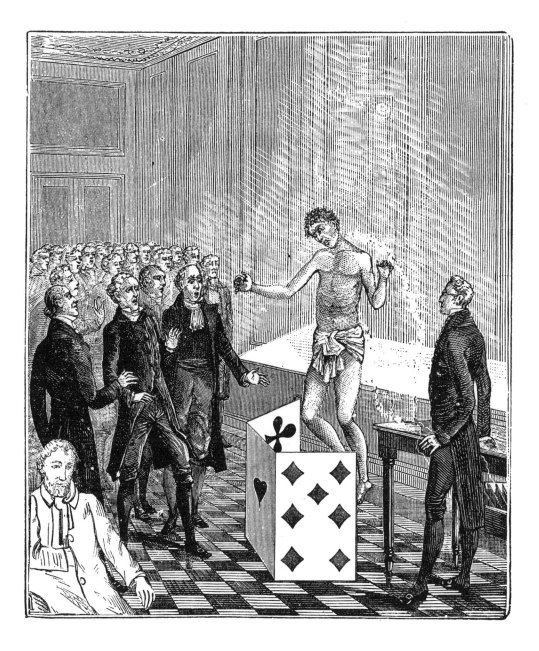

Saint Lazarus gloriously resuscitated from the camel dung.

Sachez que,

de mémoire d'homme, *La Femme* 100 *têtes* n'a jamais eu de rapport
avec le fantôme de la repopulation.
Elle n'en aura pas : plutôt se faire macérer dans la rosée
et se nourrir de violettes glacées.

Be advised that,

in the memory of man, the hundred headless woman never had a rapport
with the phantom of repopulation.
Nor will she: rather would she be crushed in the dew and feed upon
frozen violets.

LAST CHAPTER

Remercions tous Satanas et soyons heureux de la sympathie qu'il a bien voulu nous témoigner.

Let us all thank Satan and be happy for the sympathy he has been pleased
to show us.

Suite.

Continuation.

Suite.

Continuation.

L'œil sans yeux, la femme 100 têtes garde son secret.

The eye without eyes, the hundred headless woman keeps her secret.

L'œil sans yeux, la femme 100 têtes garde son secret.

The eye without eyes, the hundred headless woman keeps her secret.

L'œil sans yeux, la femme 100 têtes garde son secret.

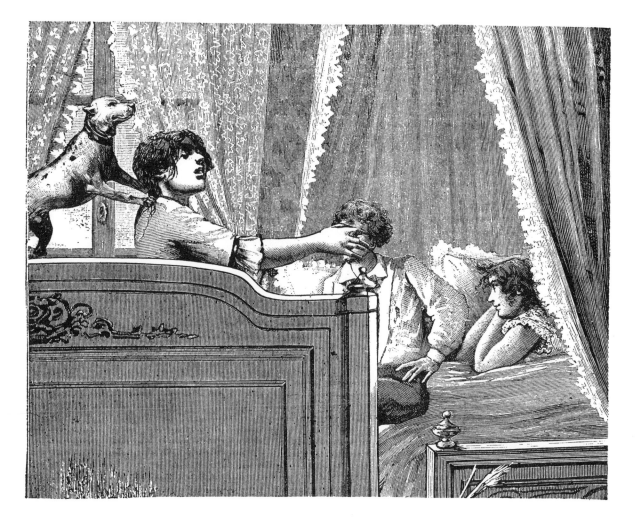

The eye without eyes, the hundred headless woman keeps her secret.

L'œil sans yeux, la femme 100 têtes et Loplop retournent à l'état sauvage
et recouvrent de feuilles fraîches les yeux de leurs fidèles oiseaux.

The eye without eyes, the hundred headless woman and Loplop all return to the savage state and cover the eyes of their faithful birds with fresh leaves.

Le Père Éternel cherche en vain à séparer la lumière des ténèbres.

The Eternal Father tries vainly to separate the light from the shadows.

L'œil sans yeux, la femme 100 têtes garde son secret.

The eye without eyes, the hundred headless woman keeps her secret.

Elle garde son secret.

She keeps her secret.

Elle garde son secret.

She keeps her secret.

Elle le garde.

She keeps it.

Rome.

Rome.

Rome.

Rome.

Paris — Marais aux Songes.

Paris—swamp of dreams.

Demandez à ce singe : Qui est la femme 100 têtes? A la manière des pères de Église
il vous répondra : Il me suffit de regarder la femme 100 têtes, et je le sais. Il suffit
que vous me demandiez une explication, et je ne le sais plus.

Ask this monkey: who is the hundred headless woman? In the style of Church Fathers
he will answer: It's enough for me to see the hundred headless woman to know.
It's enough for you to demand an explanation, not to know.

Loplop, le sympathique anéantisseur et ancien supérieur des oiseaux, tire quelques
balles de sureau sur quelques débris de l'univers.

Loplop, the sympathetic demolisher and former Bird-Superior, fires a
round of juniper berries at the debris of the universe.

Fin et suite.

End and continuation.